Calhoun

EYE OPENERS

Food

BLACKBIRCH® PRESS

San Diego • Detroit • New York • San Francisco • Cleveland
New Haven, Conn. • Waterville, Maine • London • Munich

© 2002 by Blackbirch Press™. Blackbirch Press™ is an imprint of The Gale Group, Inc., a division of Thomson Learning, Inc.

Blackbirch Press™ and Thomson Learning™ are trademarks used herein under license.

For more information, contact
The Gale Group, Inc.
27500 Drake Rd.
Farmington Hills, MI 48331-3535
Or you can visit our Internet site at http://www.gale.com

ALL RIGHTS RESERVED
No part of this work covered by the copyright hereon may be reproduced or used in any form or by any means—graphic, electronic, or mechanical, including photocopying, recording, taping, Web distribution or information storage retrieval systems—without the written permission of the publisher.

Every effort has been made to trace the owners of copyrighted material.

Photo credits: all photos © PhotoDisc except pages 4, 6, 12 © CORBIS

LIBRARY OF CONGRESS CATALOGING-IN-PUBLICATION DATA

Nathan, Emma.
   Food / by Emma Nathan.
      p. cm. — (Eyeopeners series)
   Summary: Introduces foods from different parts of the world, including sushi, sweet dates, and olive oil.
   Includes bibliographical references and index.
   ISBN 1-56711-599-3 (hardback : alk. paper)
   1. Food—Juvenile literature. [1. Food.] I. Title.

TX355 .N38 2003
641.3—dc21
                                                           2002012467

Printed in United States
10 9 8 7 6 5 4 3 2 1

Table of Contents

Morocco 4-5
North Korea and South Korea 6-7
United States 8-9
Japan 10-11
Egypt 12-13
Mexico 14-15
China 16-17
Dominican Republic 18-19
Greece 20-21
Ecuador 22-23

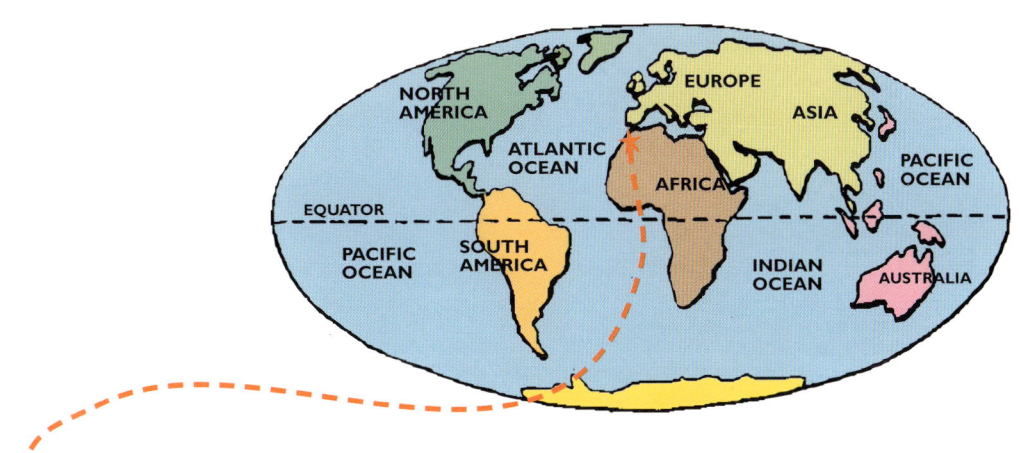

MOROCCO (maw-ROCK-ko)

Morocco is on the continent of Africa.

Many traditions in Morocco come from the Arab world.

Moroccans make a special bread called *ksra* (KISS-rah).

Ksra is a flat bread. It is spiced with anise. Anise tastes like licorice.

Ksra is usually eaten warm.

◀ **Man with ksra bread**

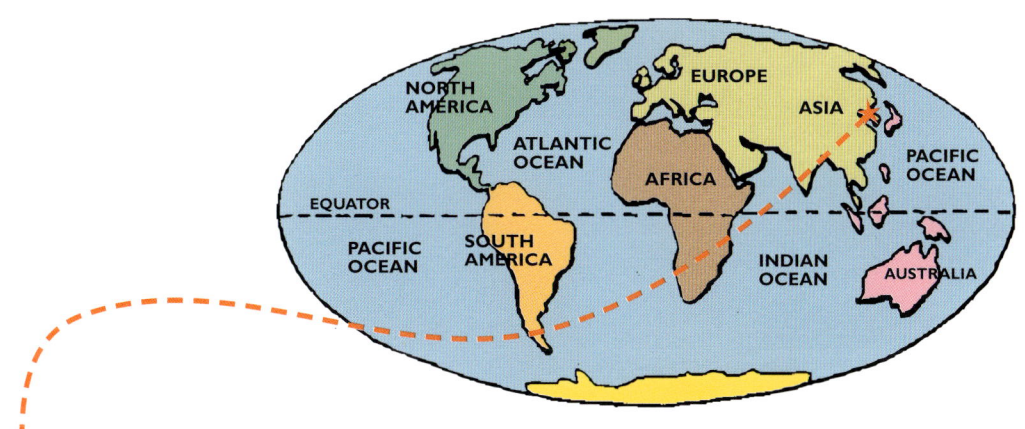

NORTH KOREA and SOUTH KOREA (ko-REE-ah)

North and South Korea are part of Asia.

The two countries are on a large peninsula. They stick out from China into the Sea of Japan.

Most of the peninsula is forest and mountain ranges. There is little land for farming.

Fish is the main food in Korea.

Dried squid and shrimp are popular snacks. Seaweed is added to soups for flavor.

◀ **Dried fish in a Korean market**

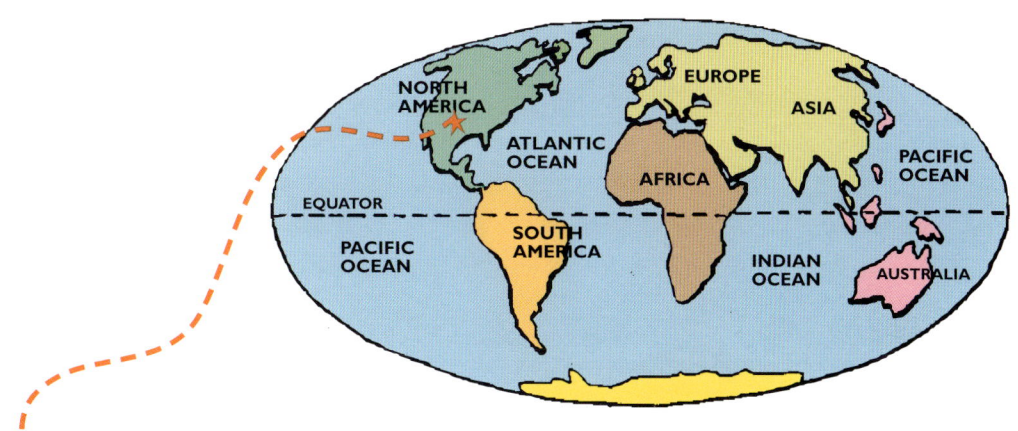

UNITED STATES (yu-nye-ted STAYTS)

The United States is on the continent of North America.

The United States has immigrants (IH-mi-grants) from many different countries.

Immigrants are people that come from another country.

Pizza is one of the most popular foods in the United States.

Italian immigrants brought traditional recipes for pizza to the United States.

◀ **Pizza is a popular American food.**

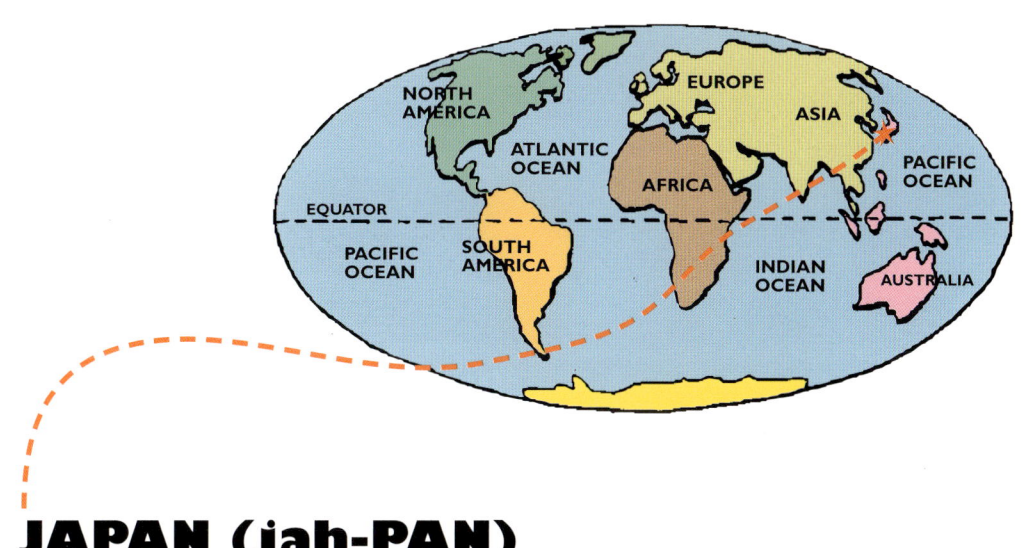

JAPAN (jah-PAN)

Japan is an island in Asia.

It is completely surrounded by the Pacific Ocean.

There is very little farmland in Japan. Fishing is Japan's major source of food.

There are many different recipes for cooking fish in Japan.

Sushi (SOO-shee) is one of Japan's most famous kinds of food. It features raw fish and rice.

◀ **Sushi is made from raw fish.**

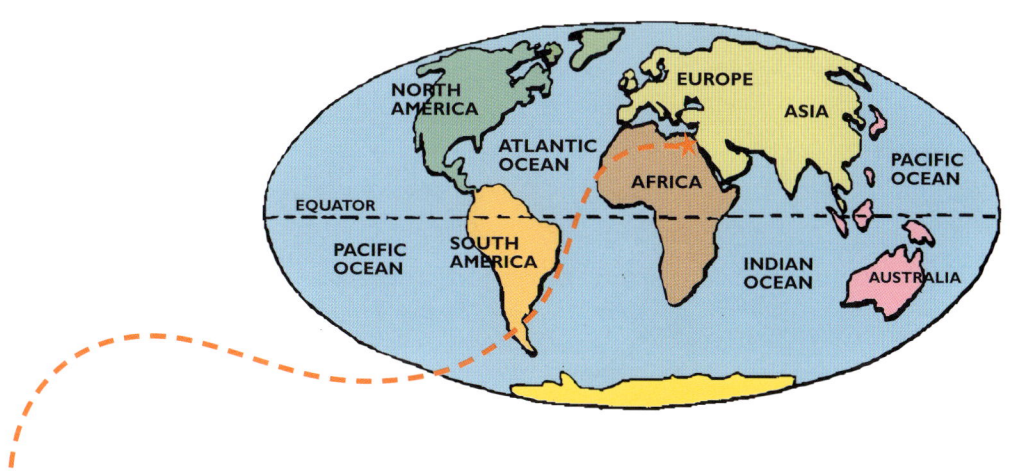

EGYPT (EE-jipt)

Egypt is part of the continent of Africa.

Much of Egypt's land is desert. Little can grow there.

Palm trees that grow dates do well in Egypt.

Sweet dates are one of the most popular desserts in Egypt.

◀ **Dried dates and other fruits in an Egyptian market**

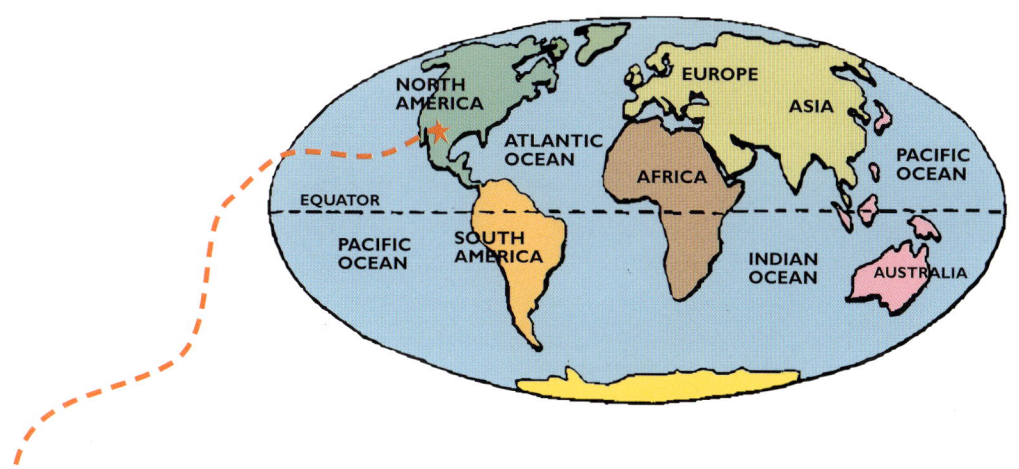

MEXICO (MEKKS-ih-ko)

Mexico is on the continent of North America.

Ancient people in Mexico were called Aztecs.

Aztecs grew cocoa beans and made chocolate thousands of years ago.

Today, cocoa beans are still an important crop in Mexico.

Some traditional recipes for chicken and other foods even use chocolate in the sauce.

◀ **Cocoa beans**

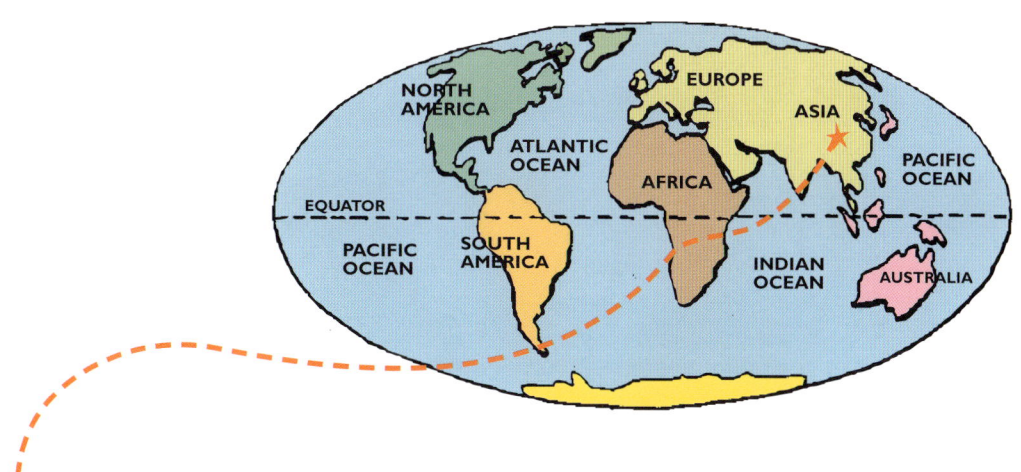

CHINA (CHY-nuh)

China is on the continent of Asia.

Tea is the traditional drink of China.

Most people in China drink tea several times a day.

There are many different kinds of tea in China.

Some of the most popular teas are green tea, black tea, and jasmine tea.

◀ Tea harvesting in China

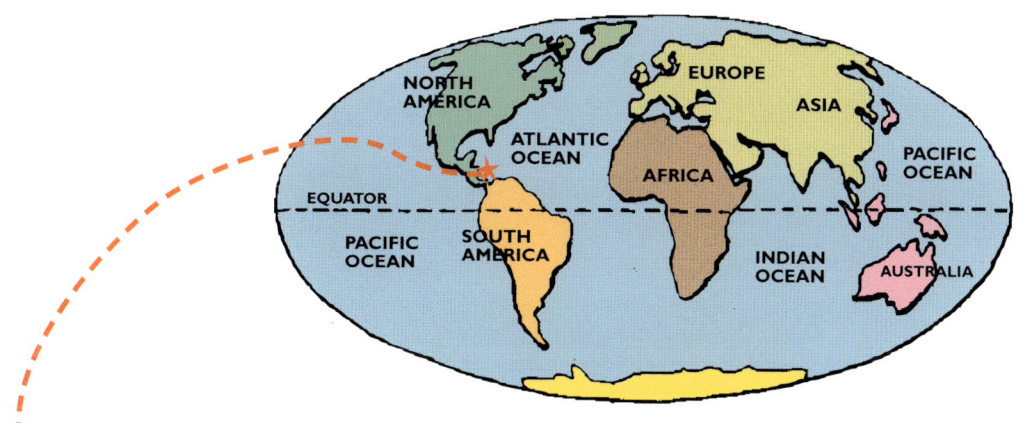

DOMINICAN REPUBLIC
(doe-MINN-i-kan ree-PUBB-lick)

The Dominican Republic is part of North America.

It is part of an island in the warm Caribbean.

Tropical fruits and vegetables grow well in the warm and moist climate.

19 kinds of mango grow in the Dominican Republic. Pineapples, bananas, and oranges also grow well there.

◀ Many fruits grow in the Dominican Republic.

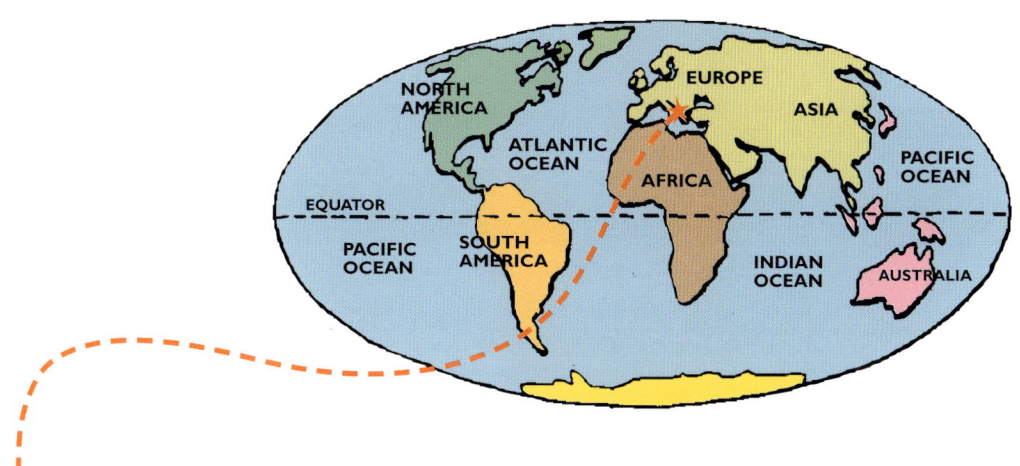

GREECE (greese)

Greece is on the continent of Europe.

Much of Greece is dry and hilly.

Olive trees grow well in the dry and hilly land.

Olive oil is used in many traditional Greek recipes.

Many traditional Greek baked goods use olive oil instead of butter.

◀ Greek olives in the market

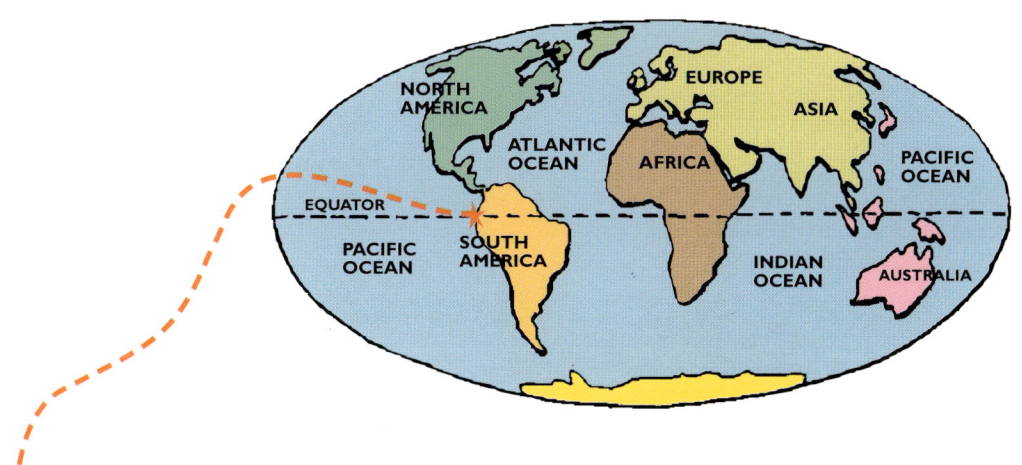

ECUADOR (EK-wah-dohr)

Ecuador is part of the continent of South America.

It is a small country that lies on the equator.

Many kinds of vegetables grow in Ecuador.

Hearts of palm is a popular vegetable in Ecuador.

Asparagus is the country's most important vegetable crop.

◀ Open-air market in Ecuador

Index

Africa, 5, 13
Arab world, 5
Asia, 7, 11, 17
Asparagus, 23
Aztecs, 15

Chocolate, 15

Dates, 13

Fish, 7, 11

Immigrants, 9

Ksra, 5

Mango, 19

North America, 9, 15, 19

Olive oil, 21

Pacific Ocean, 11
Pizza, 9

Sea of Japan, 7
South America, 23
Sushi, 11

Tea, 17

For More Information

Websites

A Culinary World Tour
http://www.gumbopages.com/world-food.html

Food Around the World
http://www.factmonster.com/ipka/A0768663.html

The Food Resource Page
http://www.orst.edu/food-resource/food.html

Books

Braman, Arlette N. *Kids Around the World Cook: The Best Foods and Recipes from Many Lands.* New York: John Wiley & Sons, 2000.

Vezza, Diane S. *Passport on a Plate: A Round-the-World Cookbook for Children.* New York: Simon & Schuster, 1997.